# Gone Fishing

by Karen Walberg • illustrated by Mark Corcoran

We get up at 4:00.

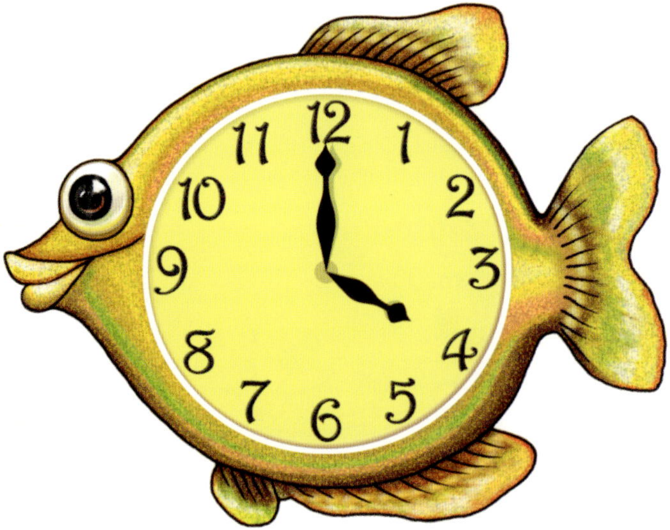


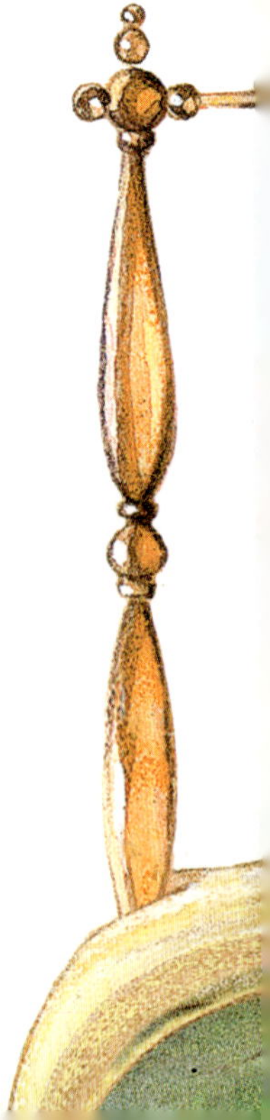

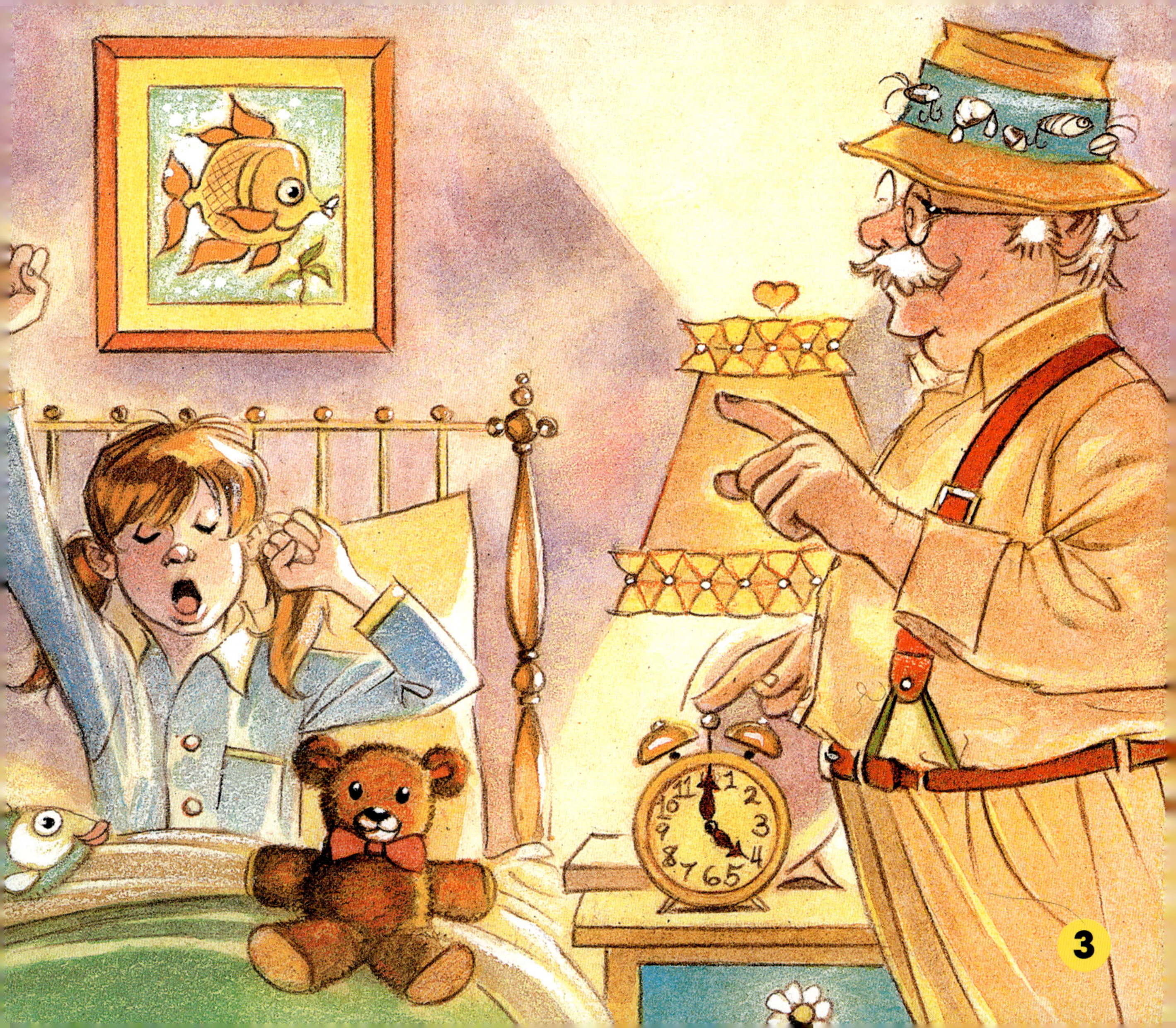

We go at 5:00.

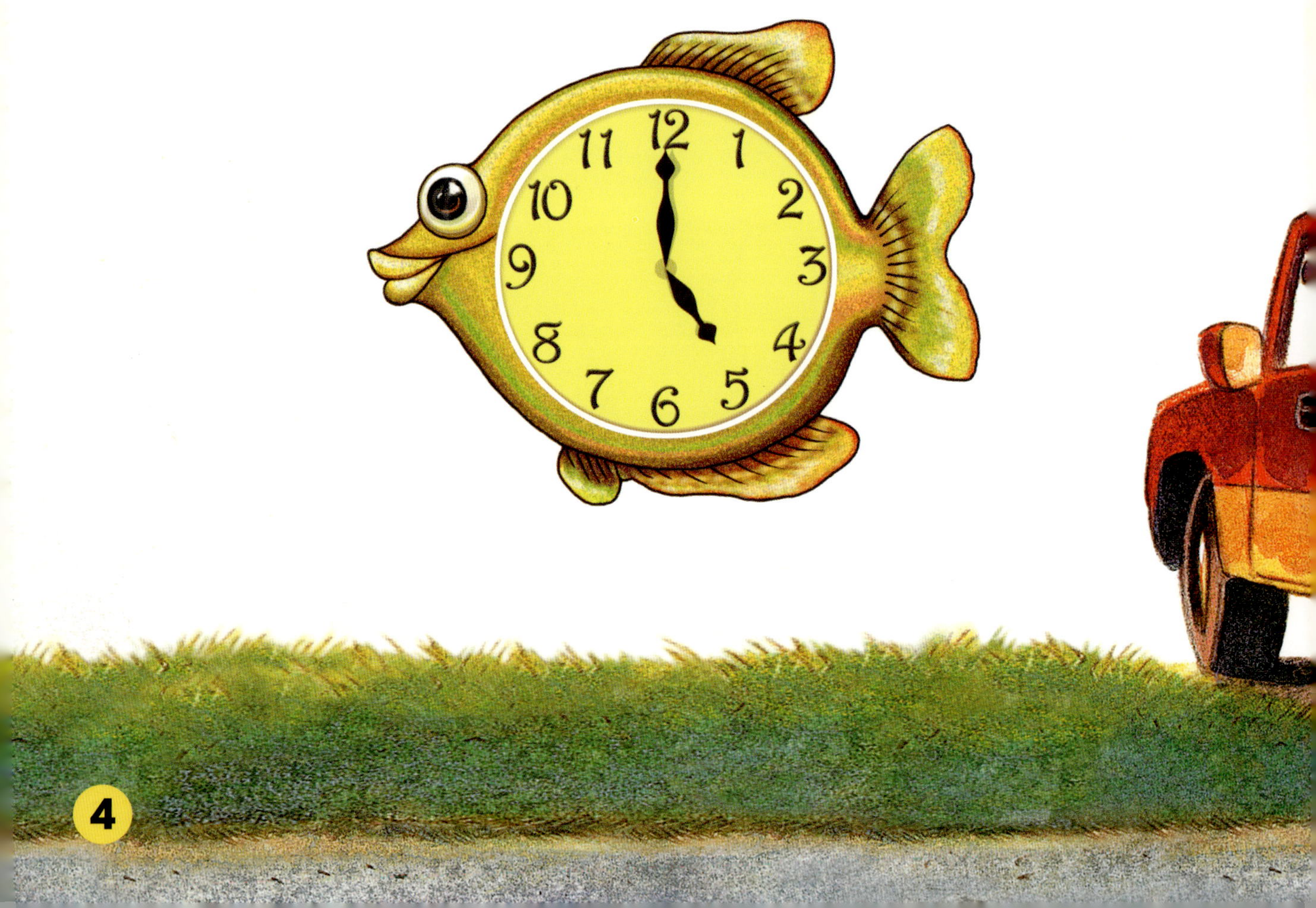

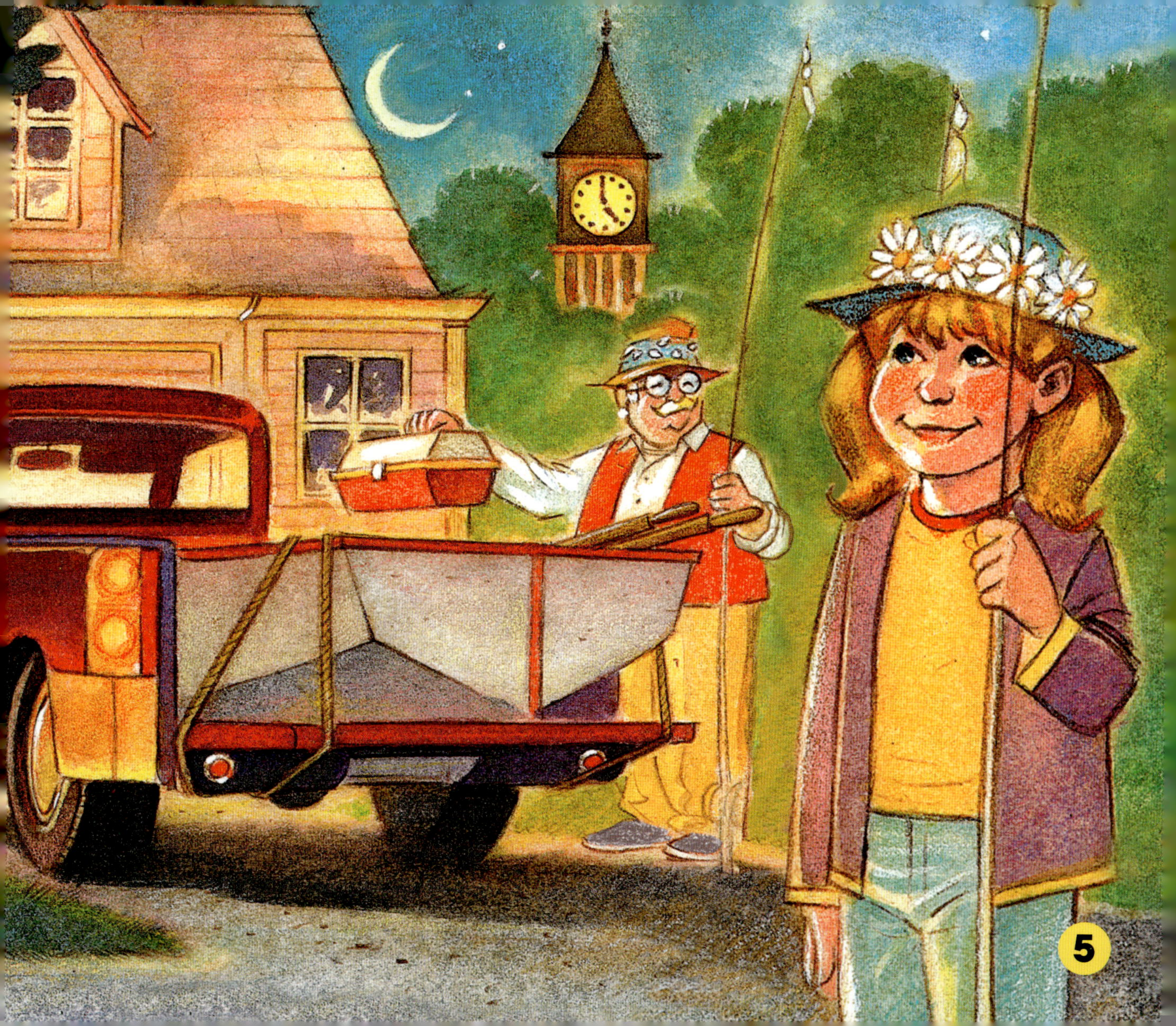

We dig at 6:00.

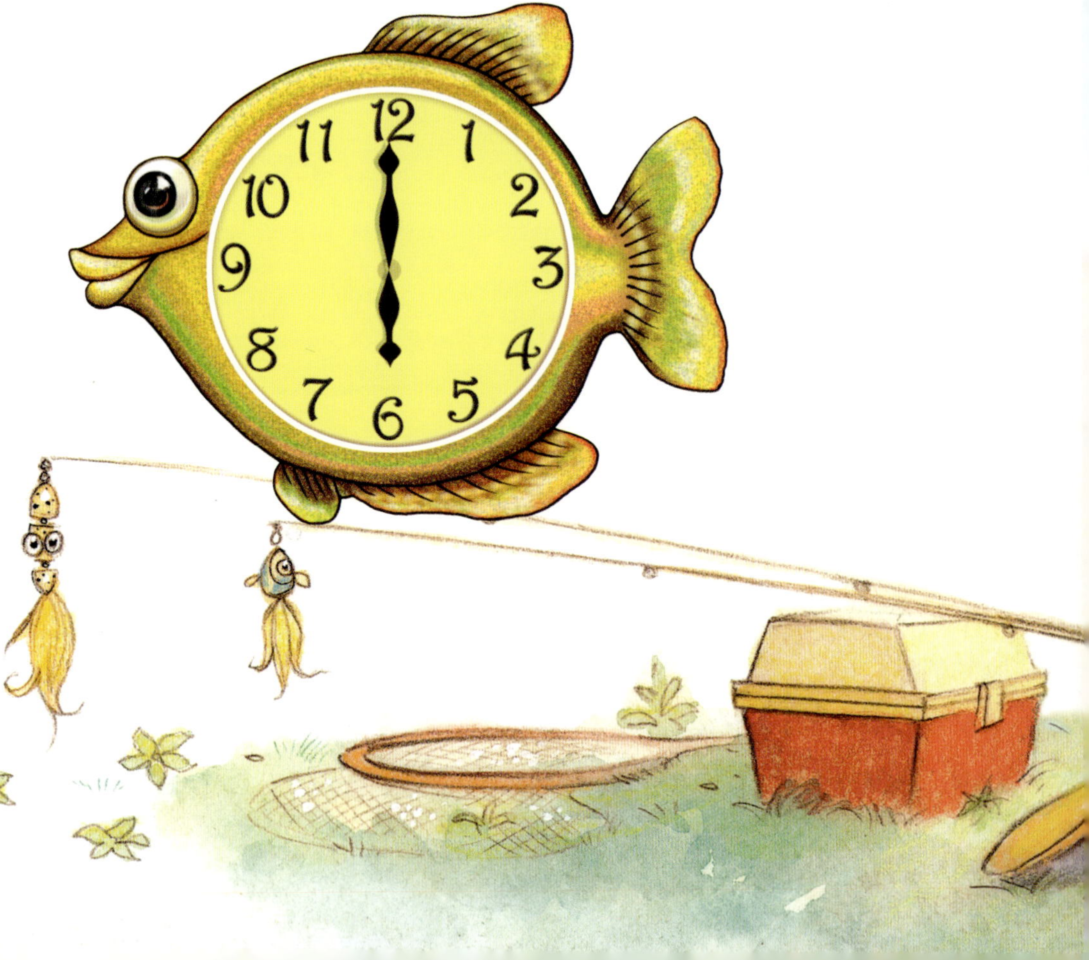
12
1
2
3
4
5
6
7
8
9
10
11

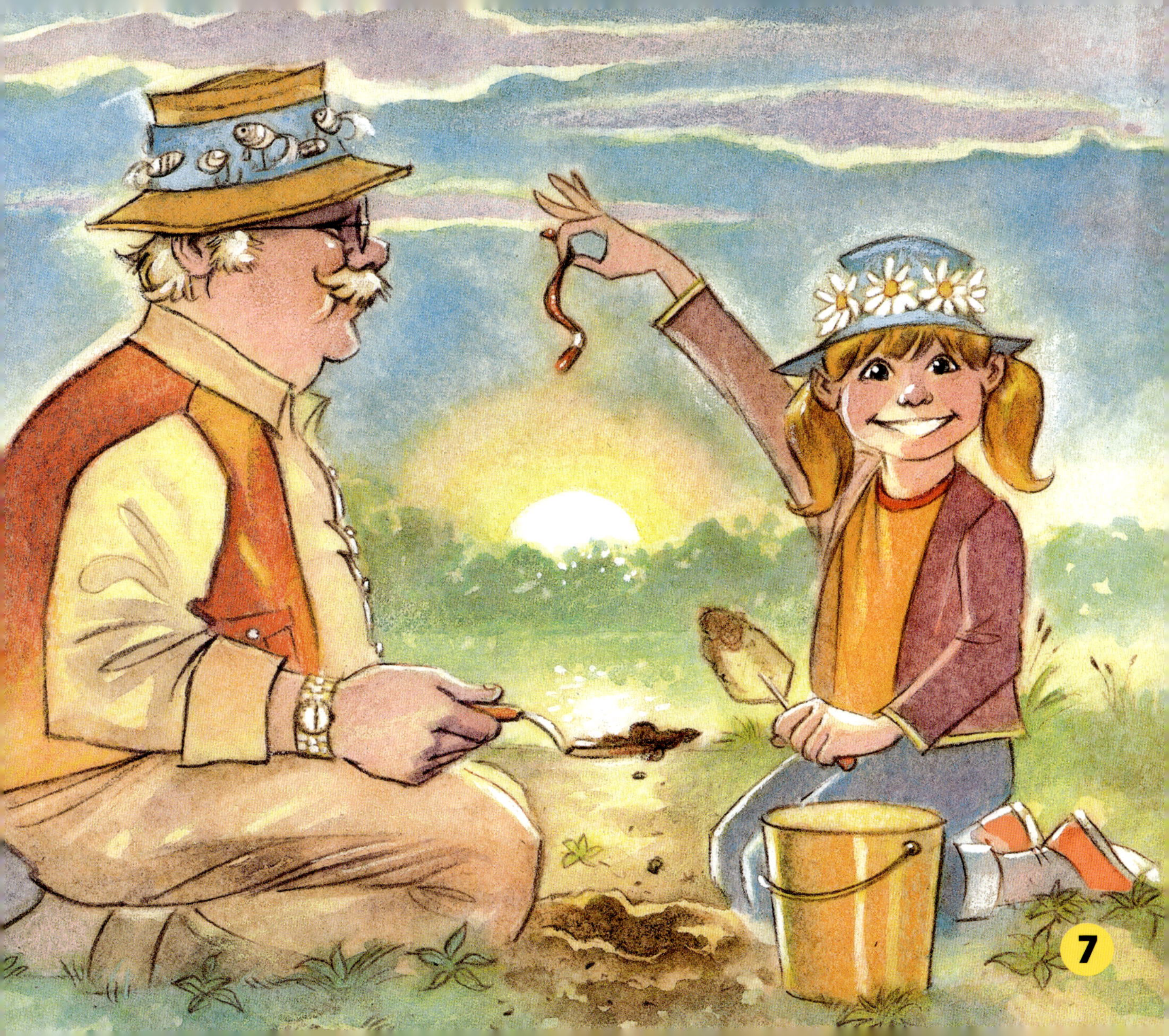

We row at 7:00.

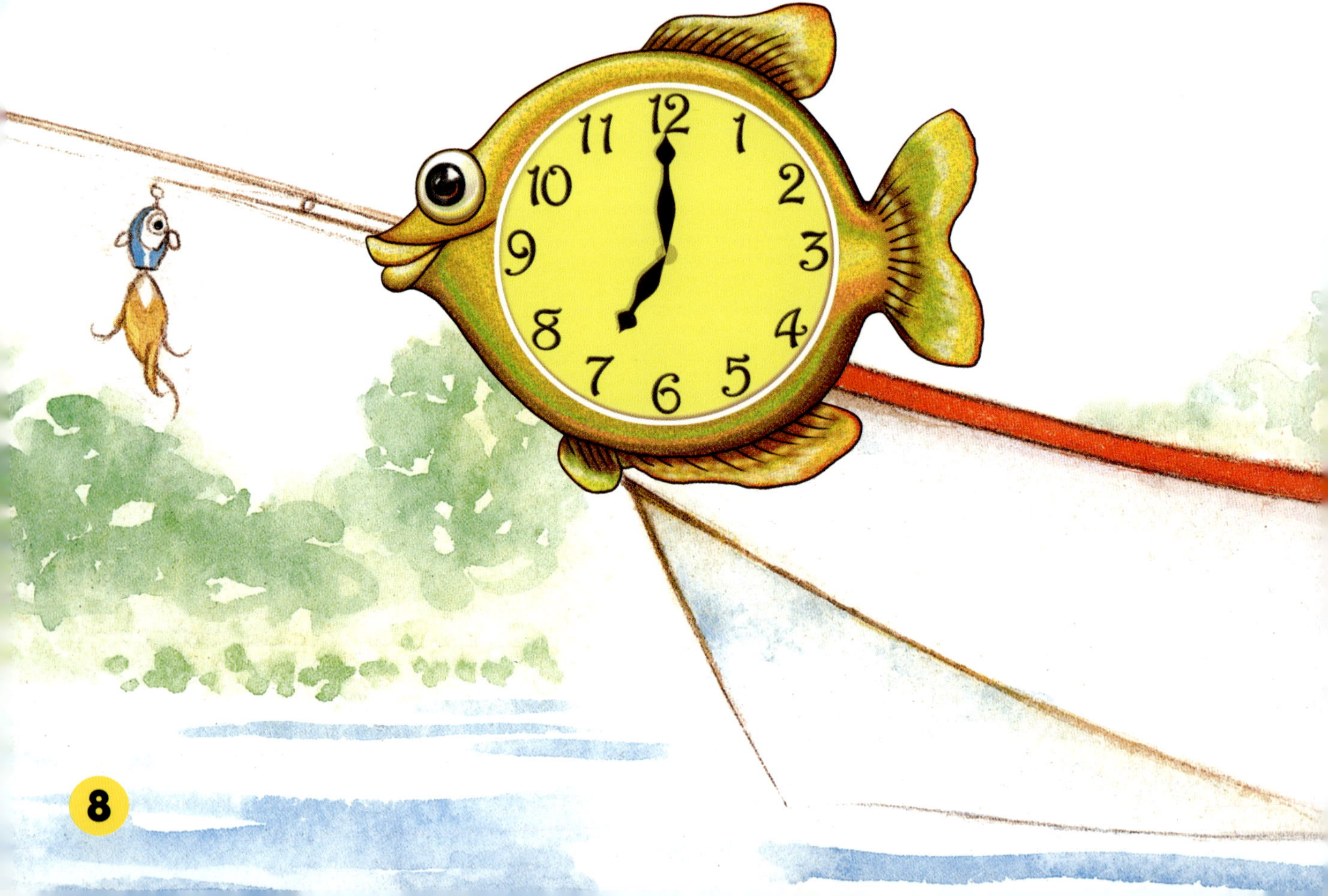

12
1
2
3
4
5
6
7
8
9
10
11

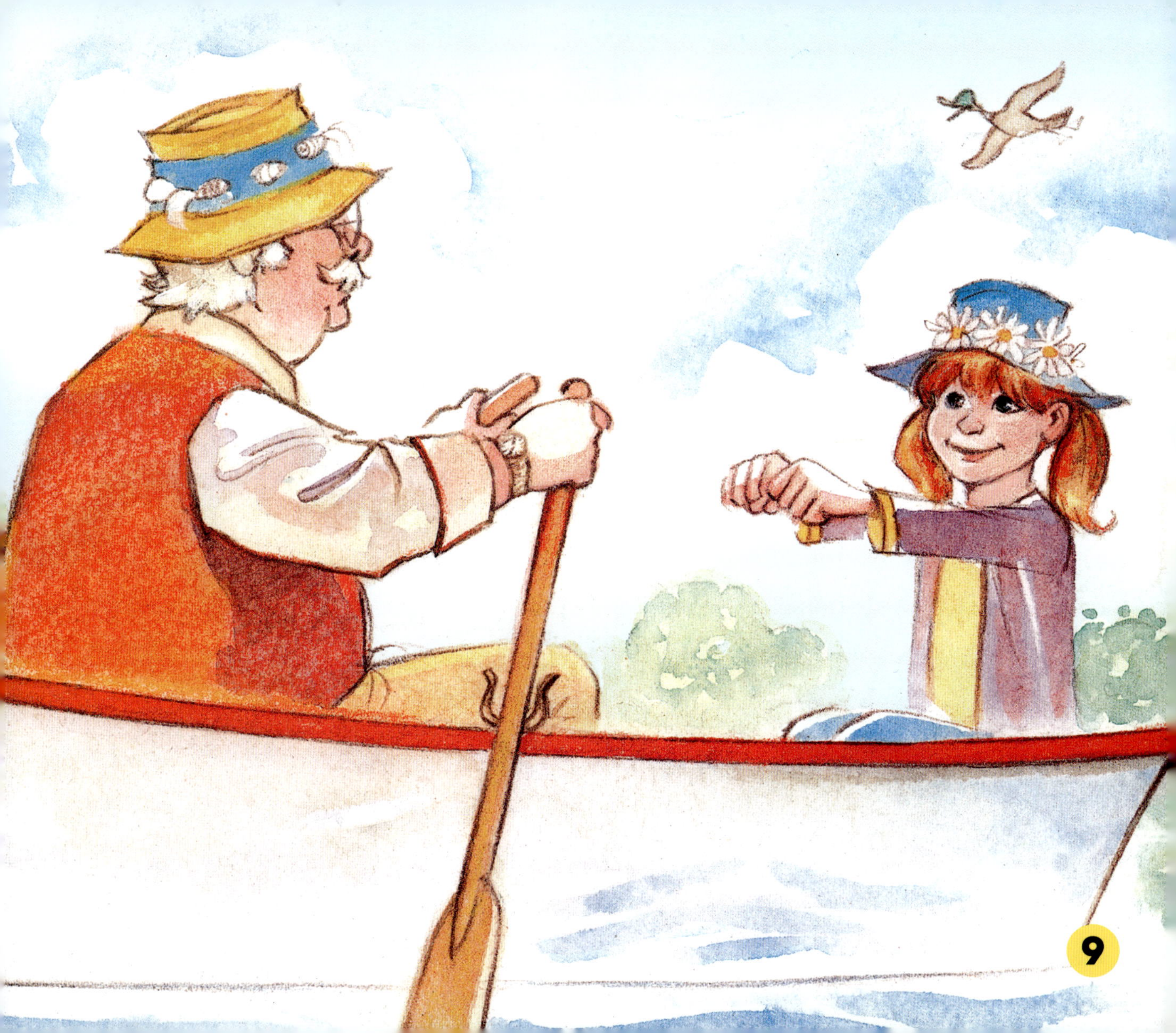

We fish at 8:00.

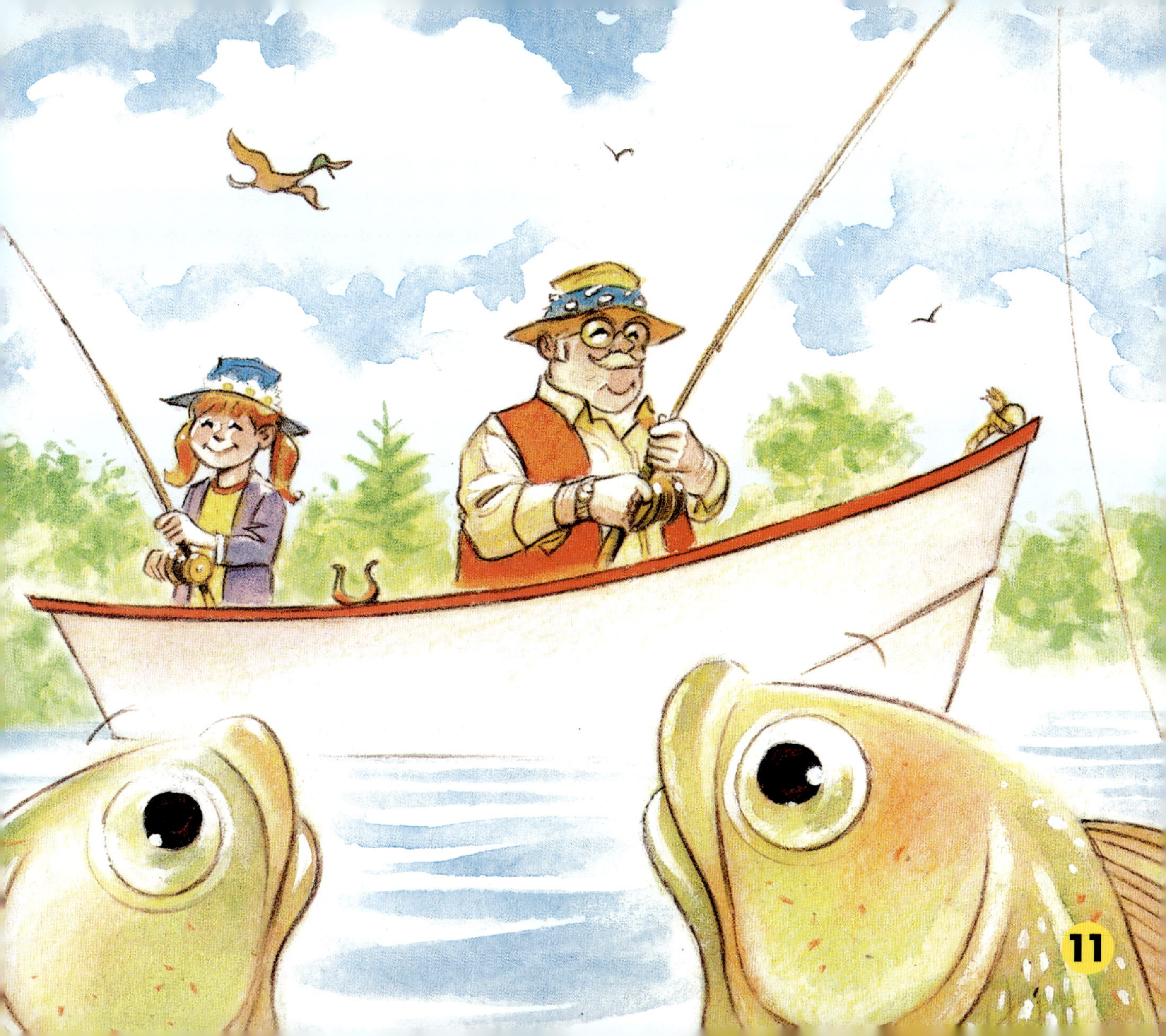

We cook at 9:00.

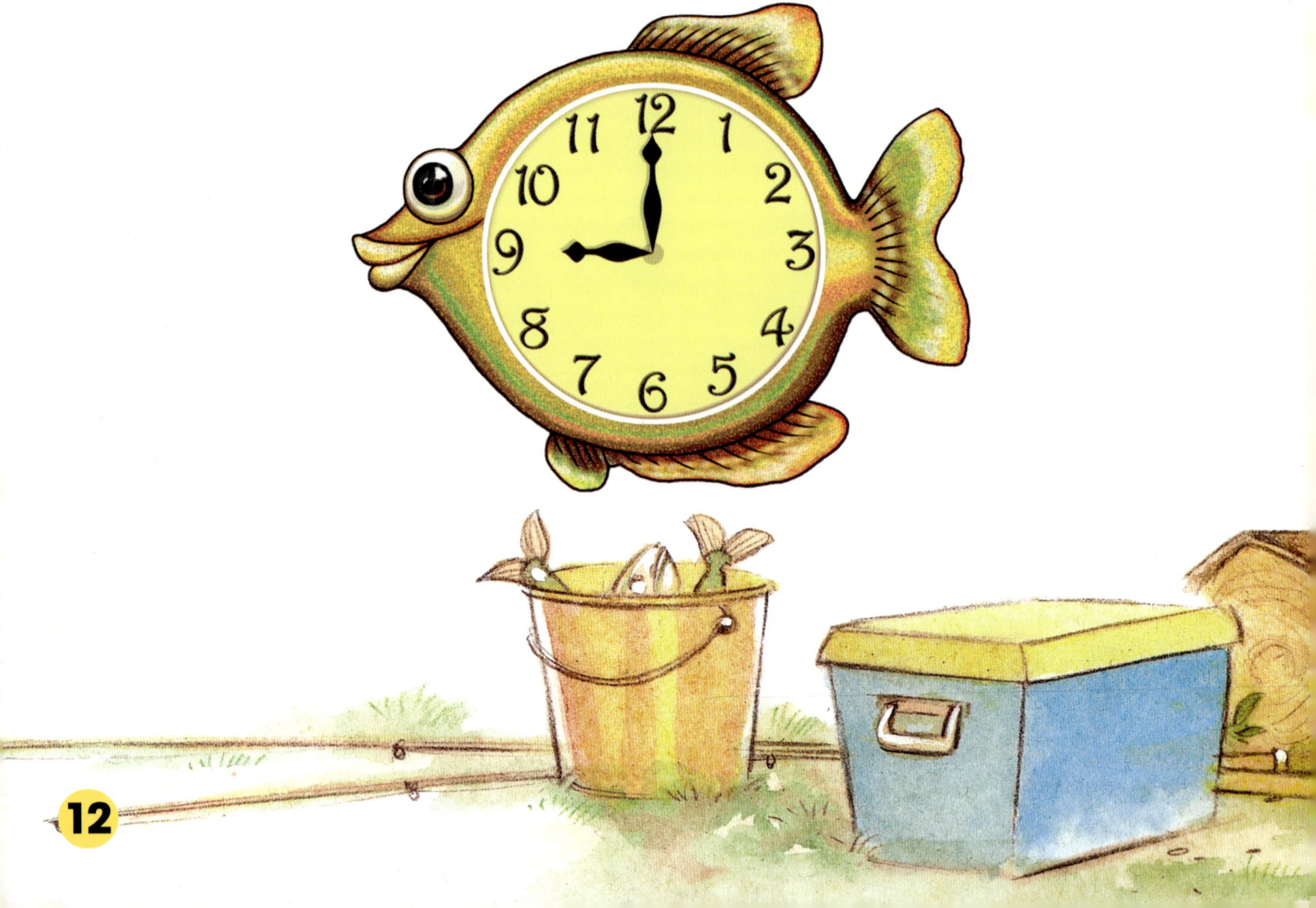

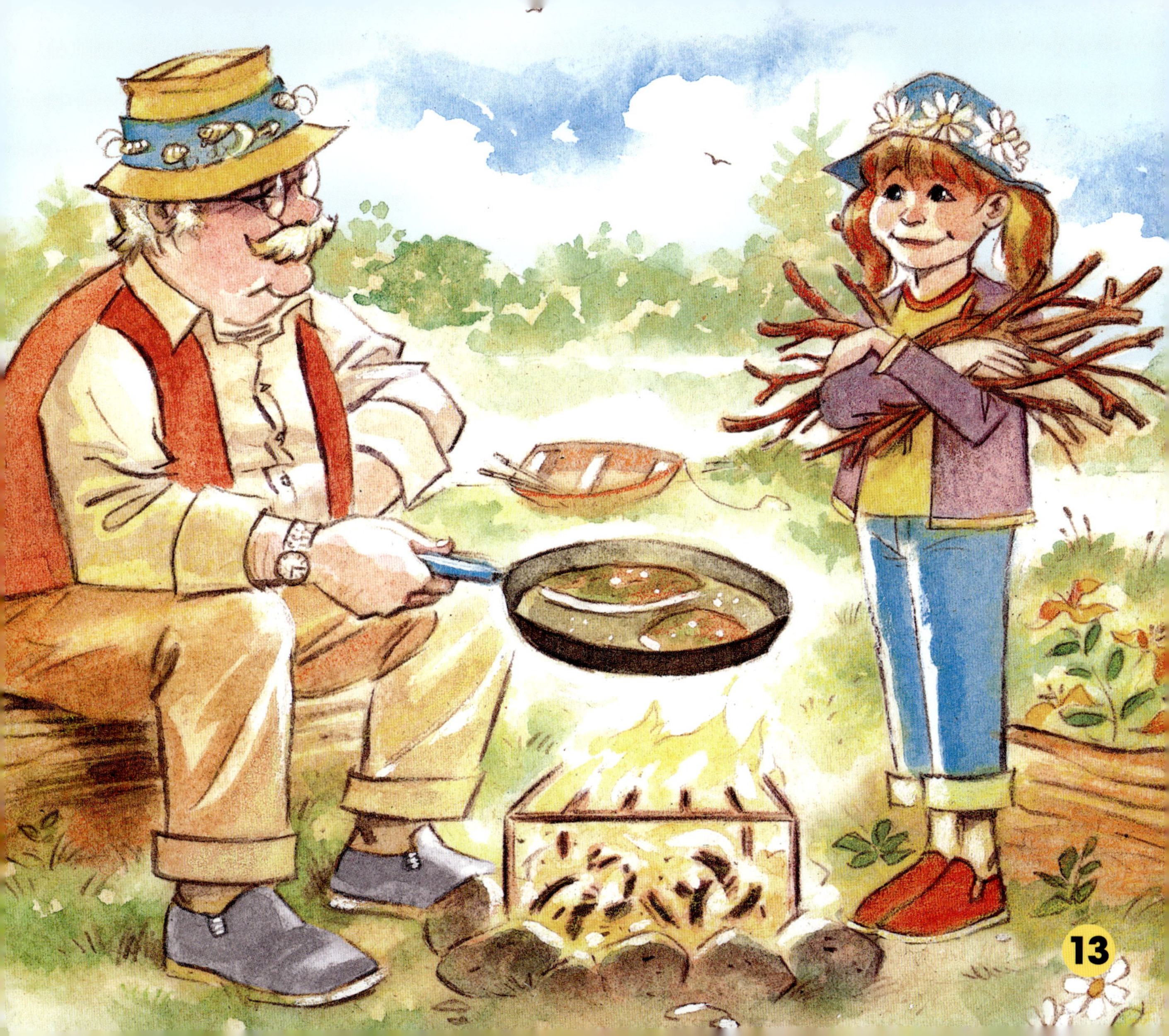

We eat at 10:00.

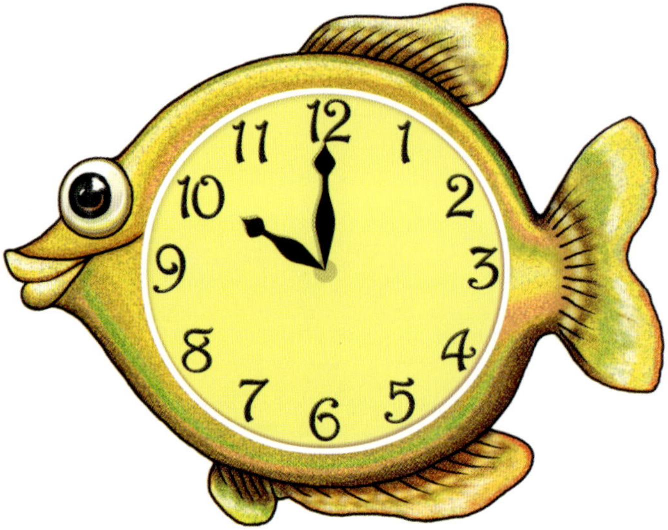

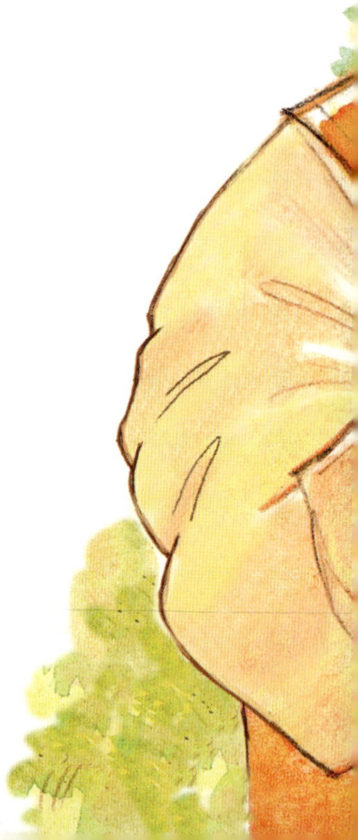

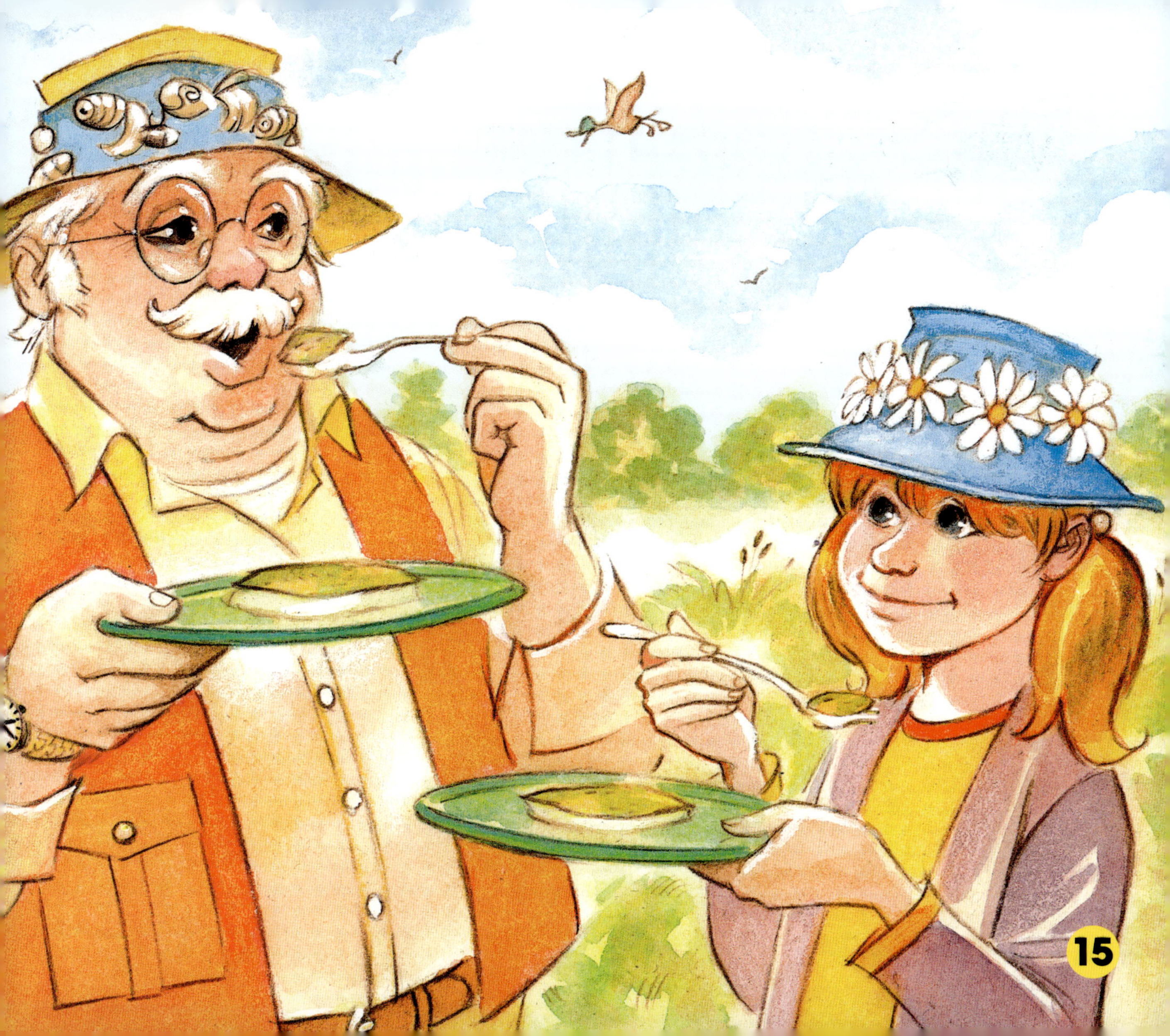

We nap at 11:00.